Bartholomew the Bossy

Marjorie Weinman Sharmat

Pictures by Normand Chartier

Macmillan Publishing Company
New York
Collier Macmillan Publishers
London

for The Boss
(You know who you are)
—M. W. S.

for Molly, Sam and Sandy,
from The Boss?
—N. C.

Macmillan Publishing Company
866 Third Avenue, New York, N.Y. 10022
Collier Macmillan Canada, Inc.
Printed in the United States of America
10 9 8 7 6 5 4 3 2 1
Library of Congress Cataloging in Publication Data
Sharmat, Marjorie Weinman.
Bartholomew the bossy.
Summary: Bartholomew Skunk is the most popular boy in
his neighborhood until he is elected first president
of the new Block Club and starts telling everyone what to do.
[1. Skunks—Fiction.   2. Animals—Fiction]
I. Chartier, Normand, date, ill.   II. Title.
PZ7.S5299Bar 1984 [E] 83-17603
ISBN 0-02-782520-5

Bartholomew Skunk was the most popular boy on
the block.

"I am popular," thought Bartholomew.

He had dozens of friends. "Too numerous to count,"
said Bartholomew.

One day Bartholomew was elected first president of
the new Block Club.

"Now I am popular and a president, too," he thought.

That night everyone on the block came to the first meeting of the club.

Bartholomew stood up. "I am your president," he said, "and I have great plans for the club. I have made a list of things that need to be done.

"Isadora Duck, write a club song and make one hundred copies. The song should have places for hand clapping, foot stamping and cheers."

"But," said Isadora.

"No buts," said Bartholomew. "Do it.

"Slim Elephant, collect the club dues, add up the money, put it in five bags, dig a tunnel under your cellar, put the bags inside and close up the tunnel."

"But," said Slim.

"No buts," said Bartholomew. "Just do those things. *Do them!*

"Neely Lion, make a club banner big enough to cover two walls and print the members' names on it in alphabetical order—with my name on top, of course."

"But," said Neely.

"No buts!" shouted Bartholomew. "I do not allow buts in my club.

"Now, Roxanne, Arnold, Evita, Lancelot and Jill, clean the clubhouse from top to bottom and from side to side. You can start as soon as the meeting is over. The meeting is over. Good night."

Bartholomew felt very important. He thought, "I like to tell my friends what to do. And they like to be told, even though they don't know it. How perfect everything is."

The next day, as Bartholomew was walking down the street, he saw Slim, Isadora and Neely.

"Slim," said Bartholomew, "you're not wearing any shoes."

"You know I never wear shoes," said Slim. "I can't find anything in my size. I'm too big."

"Well, find something," said Bartholomew.

"I will be pinched and squeezed," said Slim. "Forget it."

Bartholomew turned to Isadora. "Lap your Popsicle before it drips, Isadora."

"I like dripping Popsicles," said Isadora. "I watch the drips drip down and I think of it as a drip race and I bet on which drip will win."

Isadora didn't lap her Popsicle.

Then Bartholomew told Neely, "Part your mane down the middle so you'll look even on both sides."

"I always part my mane on the side," said Neely. "Why don't you tell the stars when to shine tonight?"

"And the moon, too?" said Slim.

"Don't tell me what to do," said Bartholomew. "I have plans for tonight. At the club meeting, I will tell everybody about the ten rules I've made up, including always calling me Mr. President. Be there on time."

That night Bartholomew went to the clubhouse, sat down in the president's chair and waited for his friends to arrive. And waited.

"How can they keep their president waiting?" he asked himself after an hour had gone by. "We need an eleventh rule. DO NOT KEEP PRESIDENT BARTHOLOMEW WAITING."

Bartholomew wrote down his new rule and kept waiting.

But no one came.

Bartholomew walked home and went to bed.

The next day nobody came to Bartholomew's house. He looked out his front window and waited.

Slim rode his bicycle right by.

Neely flew his kite right by.

Bartholomew changed windows. From his side window, he saw Isadora running on the next street. She had a dripping Popsicle in her hand. From his back window, Bartholomew saw Arnold, Rita, Edgar, Rudolph, Nigel and Melanie going past his house.

Bartholomew sighed. "Now I can count all my friends, and they add up to zero. I am the most unpopular boy on the block. I wonder why."

Bartholomew went to see Fabian Owl, who lived in the tree at the end of the block. Fabian had graduated from five colleges, and always wore turtleneck sweaters.

"Fabian must know something," thought Bartholomew. He knocked on Fabian's tree.

"Hello, sonny," Fabian called down. "Come on up."

Bartholomew climbed up.

Fabian was eating radishes while he knitted a sweater.

"I have a problem," said Bartholomew. "All of a sudden I have zero friends."

"So I've heard," said Fabian, clicking his knitting needles.

"But I don't know why nobody likes me any more," said Bartholomew.

"I will help you find out," said Fabian. "First, go home and eat nine radishes. Then hop around the block backward five times. Then read the telephone book from A to L. Then put on an ugly hat. Then come back."

"Why should I do those things?" asked Bartholomew.

"Don't ask questions, sonny," said Fabian. "Just do those things. *Do them!*"

Bartholomew left. "What a disagreeable owl! I hope his sweater unravels and his radishes mold."

But Bartholomew went home and ate nine radishes. "I never knew how very much I hated radishes until just now," he said, as he hopped backward around the block once. Twice. Three times. "I hate hopping backward almost as much as I hate radishes." But Bartholomew hopped backward around the block two more times.

Then he got a telephone book and opened it. He started to read. "'AAAAAA Action Company. AAAAAA Fish Factory. AAAAAA Laundry.' Boring. Boring. Boring!" But Bartholomew read on. And on. "'AAA Appliances. AAA Attic Fans.'"

Then he shouted, "A pox on AAA Appliances and AAA Attic Fans and all the A's and the whole telephone book! I will *not* do this. And I will *not* put on an ugly hat. But I *will* go back and tell Fabian Owl what I think of him. Which isn't much!"

Bartholomew ran to Fabian's house. "Stop knitting!" he said. "Stop eating radishes! Just listen to me!"

"Don't tell me what to do, sonny," said Fabian.

"Don't tell *me* what to do," said Bartholomew. "You're just a bossy old owl!"

"Right!" said Fabian, as he kept on knitting and eating. "And you've become a bossy young skunk. That's why you've got zero friends. And now you know."

"Oh," said Bartholomew, who suddenly knew.

"It's never too late to learn things, sonny," said Fabian. "Want to learn how to eat radishes properly? How to knit without dropping a stitch?"

"Not now," said Bartholomew. And he went home.

The next day Bartholomew waited for Slim to ride by on his bicycle. "Slim," he said, "I want to talk to you about your shoes."

"Not again," said Slim. "I don't want to be squeezed and pinched."

"Right," said Bartholomew. "You know what's right for you."

"Glad and astonished to hear you say that," said Slim. He got off his bicycle and played coin flips with Bartholomew.

Then Bartholomew went to the playground where Neely Lion was on the swings. "Neely, I have been thinking about the part in your mane. It's really your mane and your decision."

"Actually," said Neely, "I might part it down the middle. I'm getting tired of combing it to the left side."

"Totally up to you," Bartholomew said.

"Great," said Neely. "Want to swing with me?"

Bartholomew and Neely took turns pushing each other on the swings.

Isadora came along. Bartholomew went up to her.

"Popsicles!" he said.

"What about them?" asked Isadora.

"Nothing about them," said Bartholomew.

"Nothing?" asked Isadora.

"Nothing," said Bartholomew. "Want to sing some songs?"

"Okay," said Isadora.

In the next few days, Bartholomew talked to all his old friends. He did not tell them what to do.

One night it was time for the club to meet again. Bartholomew went to the clubhouse. "I hope I won't be lonesome," he thought as he sat down in the president's chair.

One by one, all of the members showed up. They talked to Bartholomew. And they listened when he talked. They even called him Mr. President.

"Everything is perfect again," thought Bartholomew.

Suddenly the door to the clubhouse opened and Fabian Owl walked in.

"Greetings, sonny," said Fabian. "I came to join your club."

Fabian walked around and introduced himself to everyone. Then he stood up in front and started to talk about radishes and knitting.

"Oh, no!" thought Bartholomew.

"Radishes," said Fabian, "are one of life's true joys. They are usually red on the outside and white on the inside. Have any of you noticed that?"

Neely yawned. Slim shuffled his feet.

An hour later Fabian was saying, "So you click your knitting needles together like this: CLICK! CLICK!"

Bartholomew wanted to yell, "Stop! Sit down! Be quiet! Leave!" Instead, he muttered to himself, "I am not bossy. I am not bossy. I am not bossy. I am not bossy...."

Fortunately, after three hours of listening to Fabian, everyone fell asleep.

And they all slept peacefully until morning.